Bowled Over!

Story by Sharon Greenaway

Illustrated by Warwick Bennett

THOMSON

NELSON

1120 Birchmount Road
Toronto, ON MIK 5GA
www.nelson.com
www.thomson.com

Text © 2003 Thomson Learning Australia
Illustrations © 2003 Thomson Learning Australia
Originally published in Australia by Thomson Learning Australia

10 9 8 7 6 5 4 3 2 1
07 06 05 04 03

Bowled Over!
 ISBN 0 1762 0114 9

Printed in China by Midas Printing (Asia) Ltd

Contents

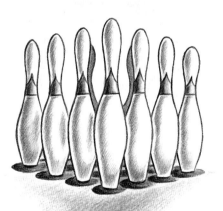

Chapter One

Whiz Bang

To:	Frank "Whiz Bang" Tippett
From:	Callum Tippett
Subject:	**Sports**

Hi Pa,

I couldn't believe it when your e-mail came yesterday! I didn't even know you had a computer.

School is okay, except for gym. I know that in every race there has to be someone who comes in last; I just wish it wasn't me *all* the time. Why can't I be good at one sport?

Now I'm a second backup for the relay on the school track team. And that's only because all the good runners were really sick when the tryouts were done.

Gotta go, Pa, dinner's ready.

Love, Callum

P.S. Why are you called "Whiz Bang"?

To:	Callum Tippett
From:	Whiz Bang Tippett
Subject:	**Try your best!**

Dear Callum,

I used to tell your father this—as long as you try your best, that's all that matters.

We've had a computer in the retirement home for ages. It's great that we're now hooked up to the Internet, too.

Love, Pa

P.S. I got the nickname "Whiz Bang" because I'm such a "whiz" at using computers.

Chapter Two

Harry Watson

To:	Whiz Bang Tippett
From:	Callum Tippett
Subject:	**The relay**

Pa,

Today I ran in the relay, dropped the baton, and made our team lose.

Even worse, Harry Watson and his friends called me *Loser!* whenever Mr. Hendley wasn't around.

I haven't told Mom because she just doesn't understand like you do.

Callum

To:	Callum Tippett
From:	Whiz Bang Tippett
Subject:	**The relay**

Dear Callum,

At least you gave it a try, and tried your best. Don't pay any attention to this Harry person; he's not worth it.

Love, Pa

To:	Whiz Bang Tippett
From:	Callum Tippett
Subject:	**Bowling**

Pa,

Just when I thought the torture was over, something else has come up.

Today, the class voted to go bowling for the end of the year party. Harry made a speech about how bowling would be so much fun. It's only because he goes bowling a lot.

I suspect he just wants another excuse to show off in front of everyone.

Callum

To:	Callum Tippett
From:	Whiz Bang Tippett
Subject:	**Bowling, eh?**

Callum,

I used to go bowling all the time. The trick, I suppose, as with anything, is to practise. Ask your mother to take you to the bowling alley for some games.

I'll go through my photos and send the bowling ones to you. Did you know that I even won a couple of trophies?

Love, Pa

To:	Whiz Bang Tippett
From:	Callum Tippett
Subject:	**Practice?**

Pa,

You think practice will help *me*? I'll probably follow the ball down the lane!

I can't wait to get those photos in the mail.

Love, Callum

To:	Callum Tippett
From:	Whiz Bang Tippett
Subject:	**Photos attached**

Hi Callum,

Not in the mail—I'm sending you the photos in this e-mail. Just double-click on the icon. The photos have scanned really well! In the background, you can see your grandma. She never missed watching me bowl, even though her arthritis stopped her from playing.

Love, Pa

To:	Whiz Bang Tippett
From:	Callum Tippett
Subject:	**Here goes ...**

Pa,

Mom said we could go to the bowling alley tomorrow night after she gets off work.

The photos are great!

Wish me luck, Callum

To:	Callum Tippett
From:	Whiz Bang Tippett
Subject:	**Practise!**

Callum,

Remember what I said in an earlier e-mail? Practise! And just try your best.

Enjoy yourself tomorrow.

Love, Pa

Chapter Three

At the Bowling Alley

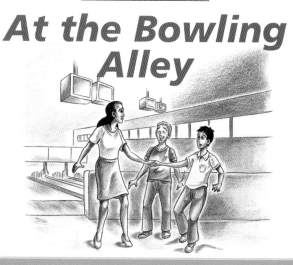

To:	Whiz Bang Tippett
From:	Callum Tippett
Subject:	**Disaster!**

Pa, you'll never guess what happened tonight! Mom and I went to the bowling alley, and guess who was there? Yeah—Harry *thinks-he's-so-cool* Watson.

I saw him and whispered to Mom that it was time for us to leave! But Harry saw us first and came over. He said it was *so* good to see me. He was acting as nice as anything because he was with his family.

The bowling alley manager's daughter, Tanya, saved me. She was really nice and helped me choose the right bowling ball. I was about to ask her for some hints on bowling when Harry walked up again. He said to Tanya that I was a really good bowler. Then he told her to keep a special eye on me. He said that she would see something *she wouldn't forget in a long time*.

Pa, I only knocked over one or two pins every time I bowled. The way Harry was carrying on, he must have gotten lots of **strikes**. He kept yelling to me from the other side of the bowling alley, "Keep it up, Callum!"

Tanya came over to watch my game, but she must have realized pretty quickly that I'd never bowled in my life before!

When we got home, Mom told me she'd had a talk with Tanya's dad. He suggested that I join a junior **league**. It starts next Tuesday night, after school. How can Mom even think that? She says the junior leagues teach you how to bowl, but I don't know. I'll be the laughing stock of everyone there!

What do you think?

Love, Callum

To:	Callum Tippett
From:	Whiz Bang Tippett
Subject:	**Junior league**

Callum,

Of course you should join! Bowling is a great sport and, believe me, being able to hit *any* pins on your first game is really good. I can still remember my first game; I only knocked down one pin.

Love, Pa

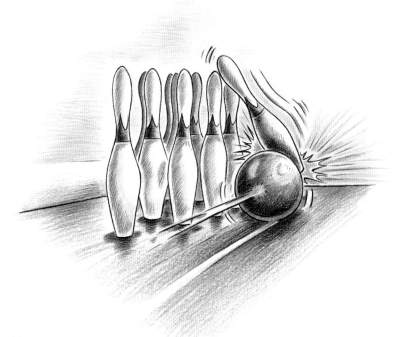

Chapter Four

Junior League

To:	Whiz Bang Tippett
From:	Callum Tippett
Subject:	**First lesson**

Pa, you'll never guess who was bowling in the junior league—Tanya!

I started to explain to her about my bowling from last week, but she stopped me. She said she knew I'd never played before because I would've known what ball to pick if I had!

And guess what? Tanya said that Harry only got those strikes because his lane had the little kids' **bumpers** up.

Then, Tanya gave me some bowling hints and I bowled a strike in the eighth **frame**! She said I was a natural. I don't know about that, but I felt fantastic!

I can't wait until next Tuesday, so I can go bowling again.

Love, Callum

To:	Callum Tippett
From:	Whiz Bang Tippett
Subject:	**Are you there?**

Callum,

I haven't heard from you lately! Does this mean you're busy bowling? It can get you like that, once you start.

Love, Pa

To:	Whiz Bang Tippett
From:	Callum Tippett
Subject:	**Guess what?**

Pa,

You're right—I've been bowling every night.

Tanya is in a tournament this weekend and she needs a partner. She asked me!

I'm really nervous. Wish me luck!

Callum

To:	Callum Tippett
From:	Whiz Bang Tippett
Subject:	**WOW!**

Callum,

You'll have a great time at the tournament. Just relax and enjoy it.

I'm sending lots of luck your way.

Love, Pa

To:	Whiz Bang Tippett
From:	Callum Tippett
Subject:	**The tournament**

Hi Pa,

We had a great time! We came in eighth out of twelve teams.

The school bowling party is just over a week away. What happens if I go to pieces in front of my friends? Then it won't be just Harry who'll never let me forget how bad I am at sports—it'll be my friends, too.

Without Tanya's help, I don't know how I'll do.

Callum

To:	Callum Tippett
From:	Whiz Bang Tippett
Subject:	**Friends**

Callum,

If they're your real friends, it won't matter.

Just have fun and enjoy yourself.

Pa

Chapter Five

A Special Present

To:	Whiz Bang Tippett
From:	Callum Tippett
Subject:	**Bowling shoes**

Pa,

The bowling shoes fit perfectly! Mom gave me the package after school. She said she'd e-mailed you my shoe size.

Thanks a lot, Pa!

To:	Callum Tippett
From:	Whiz Bang Tippett
Subject:	**Tomorrow**

Callum,

I sent the shoes as a reminder that I'll be thinking of you tomorrow.

Love, Pa

Chapter Six

Bowled Over!

To:	Whiz Bang Tippett
From:	Callum Tippett
Subject:	**Bowled Over!**

Pa,

Wait until you read this!

At school today, Harry came up to me hissing the usual *Loser!* And this time, he knocked my backpack out of my hands and my bowling shoes fell out. He started waving them in the air, yelling *Special shoes!* But everyone else thought the shoes were cool.

Bowled Over!

When we got to the bowling alley, my team was placed in the lane next to Harry and his team. It was Harry, Carly, and Brett versus me, Foong, and Nick.

Just as the game was about to start, Harry jumped up and ran over to the counter. He spoke to Tanya's dad, who shook his head. Harry was white-faced when he came back. I wondered if he was asking about using the bumpers.

Carly scored an eight and then cleared the remaining pins.

Foong's first shot was a **gutter ball**, but her second shot hit three pins.

Brett scored a two and then a three.

Nick scored a six and then a zero.

Then it was Harry's turn. He threw the ball straight into the gutter! On his second shot, Harry ran down the lane, throwing the ball really hard. This time, it sailed high into the air and landed with a huge thud in the next lane!

Carly and Brett slid down in their seats as Harry ran back up the bowling lane and then kept on running, straight for the washroom!

Then it was my turn.

I got a strike! And guess who was watching? Tanya!

Foong and Nick were as excited as I was. They were yelling and cheering as I walked back to my seat.

Pa, I ended up scoring my first one hundred and fifty game!

Tanya came over and gave me a pass for two free games.

I'll keep them for the next time you visit me.

Love, Callum

To:	Callum Tippett
From:	Whiz Bang Tippett
Subject:	**Congratulations!**

Congratulations, Callum, I'm proud of you!

Hey, who knows, you may be able to teach me a trick or two!

Love, Pa

Glossary

bumpers   barriers that run the full length of the two gutters. When in use, it is less likely that the ball will go into the gutter, and so every ball bowled should knock over at least one pin.

frames   a game of bowling is divided into ten sections or "frames"

gutter ball   when a ball is bowled and it goes down into the gutter and misses all the pins

league   when people join a team and regularly bowl against other teams, this is known as bowling in a league

strike   when the first bowl of a frame knocks over all ten pins